This book belongs to

★ ·· ★

Written by Nick Ellsworth
Illustrated by Veronica Vasylenko

This is a Parragon Book
This edition published in 2004
Queen Street House
4 Queen Street
Bath
BA1 1HE, UK

Printed in China
ISBN 1-40540-959-2

Ballerina's Magical Shoes

Written by Nick Ellsworth ★ Illustrated by Veronica Vasylenko

p

Lily the ballerina was hurrying to the theatre. Today was the day of the grand ballet. Lily was dancing with her friends Wanda, Amber and Tilly. They were all looking forward to dancing with Fleur.

Fleur was the Prima Ballerina and everyone loved her, especially Lily.

"Fleur is such a wonderful dancer," sighed Lily. "I wish that I could dance like her one day."

Fleur always danced in a magical pair of silver ballet shoes. Only the Prima Ballerina could wear them. They would not work properly if anyone else wore them.

They all loved to dance with
Fleur, and watched her closely
as she performed a perfect plié,

a beautiful arabesque,

and a stunning pirouette.

As the first dance ended, everyone clapped as the
dancers followed Fleur off stage. They hurried to
change their costumes for the next dance.

Suddenly, Fleur appeared in her bare feet, looking very upset.
"Something terrible has happened!" Fleur exclaimed. "I took off my silver
ballet shoes to retie them and now they have gone. I won't be able to
dance again until they are found."

"You mustn't worry," said Lily kindly. "We'll get them back for you."

"I'll look in the woods," said Wanda, hurrying out of the door.

"I'll look in the meadow," said Amber, as she ran off quickly.

"I'll look by the garden," said Tilly, dashing after her friends.

"We'll find the shoes in time for the next dance," Lily promised.

As Lily wondered which way she should
go, she spotted a raven flying towards
the wood. She could see something
silver dangling from its beak.

"The silver shoes!" gasped Lily.
"I'll have to run fast to keep up
with that raven."
And she ran after it.

Meanwhile, the ballet
shoes grew too heavy
for the raven.
They fell from its beak.
The shoes dropped right in
front of Wanda who was
searching the woods.

"The magical shoes!" she
said. "How beautiful they
are. I'll just try them on
quickly."

But, as soon as Wanda put on the magical shoes, a strange thing happened. She danced a plié.
She pliéd up and down and up and down, until she realised she couldn't stop.
"Help me someone!" she cried, as she danced faster and faster.
Not far away, Lily could see her friend bobbing up and down in the distance.
"I hope Wanda's all right," she thought, hurrying towards her. But poor Wanda pliéd out of the woods and into the meadow.

Wanda's legs were so tired she couldn't dance any more,
and fell flat on her back into a nearby bush.
"Are you all right?" asked Amber, who had been searching the meadow.
"Yes thanks," puffed Wanda. "But please help me take these shoes off."
Amber pulled off the magical ballet shoes and gazed at them.
"They're so beautiful," she said. "I'm sure no-one would mind if I tried
them on quickly." Not far off, Lily was rushing through the woods, trying
to catch up as fast as she could.

Amber tried on the magical shoes and
she danced a perfect arabesque.
"I never knew I could arabesque so well!" she thought. Then she
did another, and another, until she realised that she couldn't stop.
"Help! I can't stop!" poor Amber called, as she danced out of the
meadow and into the garden.

By this time, Lily had caught up with Wanda
and helped her out of the bush.
"Where are Fleur's ballet shoes?" she asked.
"Amber tried them on, and now she can't
stop dancing," puffed Wanda.
"Quick, we must follow her," cried Lily rushing off.

Amber was so dizzy from dancing that she ended up
in the fountain with a large splash.
"Help me out of here, someone!" she shouted, splashing around. Luckily,
Tilly was nearby and ran to help. But when she saw
the silver shoes lying on the ground, she just couldn't resist
putting them on.
"They're so beautiful," she said. "I'm sure no-one would mind
if I tried them on quickly."

But when Tilly tried on the magical
shoes a strange thing happened.
She started to pirouette, around and
around...

"Wheee...this is fun!" exclaimed Tilly.
"I never knew I could pirouette so well!"

But then she began to spin faster and faster,
and realised that she couldn't stop.

Lily and Wanda reached
the fountain and helped
Amber out of the water.
"Where are Fleur's ballet
shoes?" asked Lily.
"Tilly put them on and
now she can't stop
dancing," replied Amber.
"We'd better follow her,"
said Lily, running on.

Poor Tilly pirouetted down the hill straight into a muddy puddle. The others caught up with her and helped her up.

Lily carefully took the precious ballet shoes off Tilly's feet. "They are so beautiful," said Lily, and she wanted to try them on too. But in her heart, she knew that there was only one person who was meant to wear them.

"Let's return the shoes to the Prima Ballerina," she said to the others. "She'll be so happy we found them."

"My shoes!" exclaimed Fleur when
Lily and the others returned.
"How can I ever thank you?"
Fleur gave Lily a silver charm in
the shape of her silver ballet shoes.

It looked just like them.
"Thank you," said Lily gratefully.
"I'll treasure it forever!"

"Now we must finish the show," said Fleur looking around at the girls. But Wanda, Amber and Tilly were in such a mess they couldn't go back on stage.

"Oh, dear!" Fleur sighed. "You won't be able to dance looking like that." Then Fleur turned to Lily with a smile. "We will dance together."

Lily danced with the Prima Ballerina. They danced a plié, an arabesque and a pirouette. And they danced so beautifully together that everyone clapped and cheered more than ever.

The magical silver charm helped Lily to dance the most beautiful dance of her life.

"I'll remember this evening for ever and ever," thought Lily, as she walked to the front of the stage, and took her final bow.